POCKET HEROES

HENRY⅛

For my wife, Diane, and the family de Staercke – who gave me the precious time to let my pen flow...
D.W.

For Claire, John, Kat, Natasha and Imogen
C.I.

ORCHARD BOOKS
338 Euston Road, London NW1 3BH
Orchard Books Australia
Level 17/207 Kent Street, Sydney, NSW 2000

First published in 2013
First paperback publication in 2014

ISBN 978 1 40831 355 8 (hardback)
ISBN 978 1 40831 361 9 (paperback)

A CIP catalogue record for this book is available from the British Library.

1 3 5 7 9 10 8 6 4 2 (hardback)
1 3 5 7 9 10 8 6 4 2 (paperback)

Printed in Great Britain

Orchard Books is a division of Hachette Children's Books, an Hachette UK company.

www.hachette.co.uk

HENRY 1/8

DAVE WOODS
CHRIS INNS

ORCHARD

Henry VIII was a larger than life king. But before that, he was only half the man he was. And before that, only a quarter. And, when he was really, really young, he was just an eighth…

Verily, he was Henry the 1/8th!

There was a time (ages ago) that was known as the Middle Ages.

(Not the Beginning Ages or the End Ages, but the Middle Ages.)

In the Middle Ages people liked all sorts. They liked Ports. And they liked Forts. They even quite liked Courts. But what they really, really liked…

Was SPORTS!

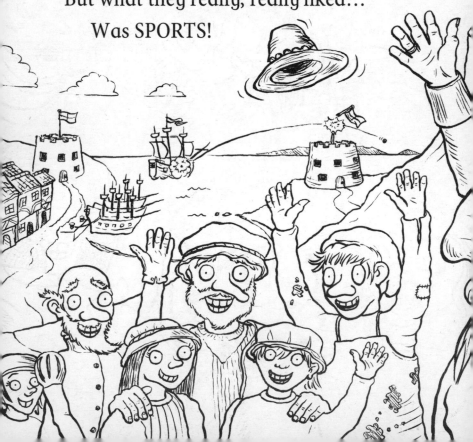

So imagine how happy the good
folk of England were when it was…
ALL-ENGLAND SPORTS DAY!

And in the Middle Ages, sport was all about one thing:
HUNTING-SHOOTING-FISHING!
(Which is actually three things, but never mind.)

In the mountains, folk would chase stags across the crags.

In the wilds, they would seek boar on the moor.

In the
wetlands,
they would
fish bream
from the
stream.

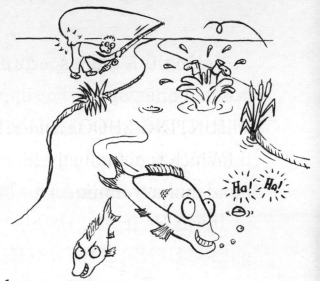

(And when they
returned, they'd find ants in their pants.)

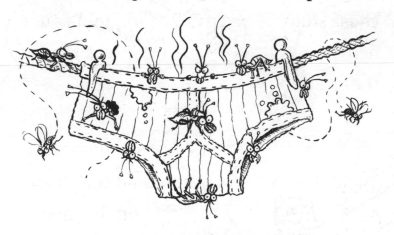

Yes, all the noblemen (and even the not-
so-noble men) loved their sport.

And on this great sporty day, so word has it, a great sporty boy appeared. A boy who was square of shoulder, but not of thinking. A young boy with action on his mind and a fraction on his back…

It was Henry the 1/8th!

"I'M HENRY THE 1/8TH, I AM, I AM. I'M HENRY THE 1/8TH, I AM!" he announced.

(See, told you it was him.)

"HEAR ME," he said to the crowd.
"I BEAR NEWS OF A NEW WAY
FOR ENGLAND TO FIND SPORTING
GLORY – AND FOR MORE THAN JUST
ONE DAY!"

"Eh? Glory in what?" said Sir
Thomas of Doubting.

"We shall win YE FIRST WORLDE
CUP!" cried Henry the 1/8th, nobly.

"What's YE FIRST WORLDE CUP?"
(It was a good question.)

"A PRIZE WORTH WINNING!"
explained Henry the 1/8th.

(It was a good answer.)

"How do we win it?" asked someone
in garb and hose. (They're fancy words
for fancy clothes.)

"BY BECOMING CHAMPIONS IN A
FINE NEW SPORT!" he explained.

"A sport of which sort?"

"A SPORT...WITH A BALL!"
said Henry the 1/8th.

"A cricket ball?"
asked Sir Freddie of
Flintlock, who loved
the little red ball.

"NO."

"A rugby ball?" asked Lord Lawrence of Di-Lally-Ally-O, who loved the oval ball.
"NOPE."

"A tennis ball?" asked Sir Andrew of Murraymintshire who loved to swat the bright green balls like flies.
"NAH."

"A cannonball?" asked Sir Francis Duckling, who loved to fire the heavy metal ball at England's foes.
"NOT LIKELY."

There was a pause…for thought.
(But no thoughts arrived.)

"I'm stumped!" said Sir Freddie
of Flintlock.

"Given up trying!" said Lord
Lawrence of Di-Lally-Ally-O.

"Deuced if I know!" said Sir
Andrew of Murraymintshire.

"Blast!" said Sir Francis
Duckling.

Then, as the crowd stared in amazement, Henry the 1/8th opened his LAD-I-DAS sports bag…

He stuck in a thumb and pulled out a plum— (er, sorry, wrong story). He stuck in his hand and pulled out something round and leathery. "VERILY, 'tis A FOOTBALL!" he announced, proudly. "IT'S ROUND!" gasped the crowd. (Then gave a round of applause.)

"TO WIN YE FIRST WORLDE CUP," declared Henry the 1/8th, "WE MUST SAIL THE LOW SEAS INTO EUROPE AND DEFEAT ALL!"

"Er, don't you mean the HIGH SEAS?" pointed out Sir Francis Duckling.

"I'll sail the HIGH SEAS when I'm taller," explained Henry the 1/8th. (Which was a fair point.)

"Won't we need a footy kit?" enquired Sir Sponsor of Ship.

"Indeed! We shall wear THREE LION CUBS on our shirts," said Henry the 1/8th, "to show we are THREE TIMES BRAVER than our opponents!"

The crowd was excited and – because there'd been talk of lion cubs – gave a little roar.

"VERILY!" roared Henry the 1/8th (who was a bit excited, too), "I SHALL PICKETH MY TEAM!"

HENRY THE 1/8TH

"Verily, here is my team of Lion Cubs – I'll play them in a 4-4-TUDOR formation!"

WILLY CATCHITT

"Our goalkeeper was Chief Head-Catcher for executions in the Tower, but gave it up when he developed a nasty case of Dropsy!"

JOHN TERRIFYING

"A great defender of the realm – spiky hair, spiky temper and spiky pants!"

"CHOPPER" HARRIS

"When I say 'On me head!' he thinks I'm saying 'Off with his head!' and makes opponents run around like headless chickens."

NORMAN THE HUNTER

"A ferocious tackler,
Norman doesn't just
bite yer legs – he bites
yer backside, too!"

Grrrrrrrr

DAVID SPECKHAM

"Played for Boychester United
at the famous Young
Trafford ground.
He's got England
tattooed on his heart!"

FRANK RAMPARTS

"Builds up attacks from midfield, gives the team structure – and makes a great wall!"

RYAN GIGGLES

"So skilful he turns tackles into tickles and makes crowds giggle with excitement – the other team won't be laughing, though!"

WAYNE PUNY

"A Great British
Bulldog of a player –
prowls and growls
till the opposition
howls!"

OLIVER CROSS-WELL

"Master of the
politics of football –
crosses equally well
from the left or
right wing!"

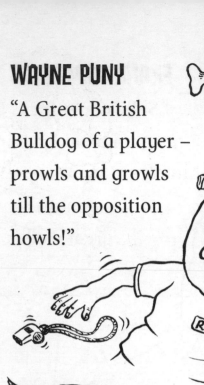

GEOFF HURTS

"Elbows of steel, knees of iron, he hits the opposition where it hurts – in the box!"

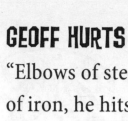

DRIBBLER THE DOG

"Dribbler's got two left feet – fortunately, he's got two right feet as well! A natural dribbler since he was a puppy!"

HOLDBRUSH THE REPORTER

"Paints the match reports after every game – he calls it painting by shirt numbers! He's also team doctor, kit man and ball boy!"

CLAUDE THE LION CUB

"Our team mascot is only 1/8th of the size of a fully-grown lion, but he can rip defences apart. Remind you of anyone?"

England's opening match of YE FIRST WORLDE CUP was against Portugal.

Henry the 1/8th's team of young Lion Cubs set off from London in the England team coach. This coach was pulled by two strong donkeys (one called Adam, the other Tony).

LUNDUN

YURP

After a brisk journey, they arrived in Dover. Dover was one of the famous medieval ports known as the 'Sink' ports. (There were five of them – two kitchen sinks, two bathroom sinks and a toilet sink.)

"Right, team," said Henry the 1/8th, "my ship's ready to board!"

"What's she called?" asked Wayne Puny.

"The *Hairy Nose*!" exclaimed Henry the 1/8th, proudly.

The *Hairy Nose*, just so you know, was the swiftest ship in the English Navy.

(The harder the wind blew the *Nose*, the faster she went.)

"Can she sail far?" asked Ryan
Giggles.

"One hundred miles to the galleon!"
grinned Henry the 1/8th.

Ryan giggled. And the team boarded
The *Hairy Nose* (which, as we now
know, was not a ship to be sniffed at).

After a lengthy voyage, they arrived in Portugal, where they came face-to-chest with the Portuguese team.

"They look big and tough," said Oliver Cross-well.

"That's because," explained Henry the 1/8th, "they're Portugeezers!"

And they were.

In the first half, the tough-tackling Portugeezers got stuck in to England.
They stuck their left boots in,
They stuck their left boots out,
In, out, in, out,
They kicked them all about.

And while the England players lay
a-groaning, a player called Do-Do-
Runaldo-Do-Do-Run-Run did just that...
He did-did-ran-ran all around them
– and scored two quick goals!

"They're kicking us off the pitch!"
moaned Frank Ramparts to the referee.

But the ref (called Turner Blindeye)
was also a ruffian (in a ruff) and
refused to rule out roughness from the
rogues...

So round the ragged wrecks the
rugged rascals ran.

The whistle
blew for
half time.

PHEW! thought the England team. The players huddled around waiting for Henry the 1/8th to work some magic. They weren't disappointed.

"If you want to get ahead," said Henry the 1/8th, "get a hat!"

"Why a hat?" asked Geoff Hurts.

"Watch," said Henry the 1/8th…

So they did.

Henry the 1/8th came out for the second half wearing a large top hat. As he went up for a header the ball disappeared (under his hat) and reappeared…in the Portuguese goal!

Henry the 1/8th did this three times (which is why when footballers score three goals it's called a 'Hat-Trick').

England won 3-2!

Magic!

The next match was the quarter-final against France!

So they set sail for France aboard The *Hairy Nose*.

But it was a dark and stormy day (followed by a dark and stormy night).

Everyone got seasick – even the ship's parrot (which is why footballers often say "I'm as sick as a parrot").

Then the night sky cleared. The ocean calmed. And they sailed across the moon's reflection on the sea surface (which is why footballers also say "I'm over the moon").

The team were hungry. They tucked into Fish & Ships.

But Willy Catchitt found a couple of beetles in his meal.

"Hmm…" he wondered. "Should I eat the big one or the little one first?"

"Always go for the lesser of two weevils!" pointed out Henry the 1/8th.

The quarter-final was in Plaster-of-Paris, in a famous stadium called Park des Prawns (with garlic mayonnaise).

The goals were made of onion bags (which is why you hear footballers saying "Stick it in the onion bag!").

Now, the French team were very adventurous...

And very cavalier...

And very daring.

So their team had no midfielders...

And no defenders...

And no goalie.

Just strikers!

It was all-out attack!

(There was only one problem…)

The…

Strikers…

Were…

On…

Strike!

(They wanted better playing

conditions.)

The ref consulted his rule (Britannia) book. There was only one thing for it. DISQUALIFICATION!

(Which is a very long word for a very short match.)

So, before the French had even kicked off – they were kicked out!

England were in the semi-final!

After the match, the French captain, Guillo Teen, got the chop.

And their vice-captain, Serge Forward, threw himself off the Trifle Tower into the river below (sadly, he had gone in-Seine).

The England team sailed into the nether regions – to play the Netherlands (that's Holland to you and me) at the Hamsterjam Stadium!

Holland were so good they were known as 'The Dutch Masters'.

And they were twice the size of the English players.

It's double Dutch to me!

And they were made
even taller by
playing in clogs.
(A clog is a small log
with a hole in it.)

And they used a large
red cheese as a football.

Oh, AND it was
snowing!

So, not surprisingly:

After ten minutes,
Holland were ahead by a header.

After twenty minutes, they were
ahead by two headers.

After thirty minutes, they were...
(You see how it was going.)

CHATTER!   BRRRRR!

Soon, Holland were winning 4-0.

The goals were all scored by a giant Dutch striker called Onmee Hedson.

At half-time, oranges were brought out (by a boy called William) and the snow was heavier than ever.

The situation looked, well…white.

The snow was thick. But Henry the 1/8th wasn't.

He disappeared into the snowstorm and came back dragging some toboggans.

"The Dutch play the ball high," he said, "so we'll play them low, with a new kind of tackle…"

"What sort of tackle?" asked Norman the Hunter.

"VERILY, THE SLIDE TACKLE!" grinned Henry the 1/8th.

Norman the Hunter, John Terrifying and 'Chopper' Harris slid into action and swept the ball out from under the Dutch team's feet.

"OFF WITH THEIR CLOGS!" cried Henry the 1/8th.

There were flying Dutchmen everywhere!

Holland's goalie, Eric Van der Half,
watched the red cheese fly past him...
five times! It was tough cheese for him.
(In fact, it was tough, tough, tough,
tough, tough cheese.)

At the final whistle, the Holland
captain, Ruud Gesture, was a sore
loser. Because his team, who played in
orange, ended up black and blue!

England were
in the final!

Finally, it was the final. England v Spain in the Bull Ring Stadium in (stark raving) Madrid.

The Bull Ring was aptly named – as the Spaniards were big bullies.

In fact, their best striker was…a bull!

(He was called Fernando Torro.)

This was unfortunate for England, who were playing in their AWAY kit – which was RED!

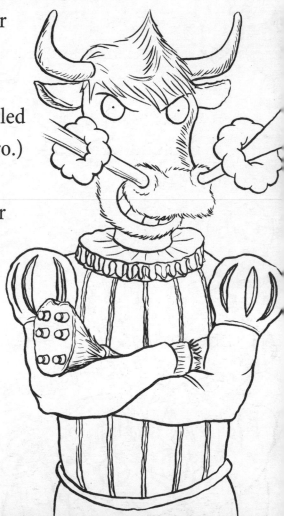

Fernando Torro saw the England kit
and went (stark raving) mad.

It was a red rag to a bull. (Obviously.)
He charged the England team! So did
the rest of the bullies.

They gave Henry the 1/8th no quarter.
Fernando Torro butted in two crosses
to give Spain a 2-0 lead.

Just before half-time, there was a fracas, when a player called Maracas scored with a tacos! (Yes, it was a delicious chip.)

The half-time whistle blew. Spain had three goals – our heroes had zero!

The England team huddled.

They were all befuddled.

And awfully muddled.

(They needed to be cuddled.)

"We need a change of tactics!"
sobbed David Speckham (whose tears
had puddled).

"Nay," said Henry the 1/8th.
"We need a change of kit!"

"Why?" asked 'Chopper' Harris.

"Because our HOME kit is made
of ARMOUR!" grinned Henry the 1/8th.

His team grinned, too.

"OFF WITH
OUR KIT!"
cried Henry
the 1/8th.

So they changed. And, in the second half, so did the match.

The bull got rumpled – as its horns got crumpled.

And the Spanish got disgruntled – as their lead got dismantled.

Henry the 1/8th's team of young Lion Cubs clawed three goals back!

The full-time whistle blew. The score was 3-3.

The final of YE FIRST WORLDE
CUP would be decided by A PENALTY
SHOOT-OUT! (Uh-oh.)

Spain took the first penalty.
Fernando Torro shot…and missed!
(He hoofed it over the bar.)

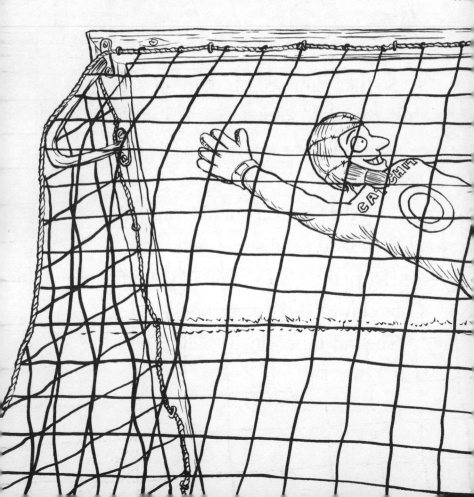

It was England's turn.

Now Henry the 1/8th launched his surprise attack...

"GIVE THEM A VOLLEY!" he cried.

The England team fired a broadside of footballs at the Spanish goal...

And scored.

(Eleven times!)

The Spanish were sunk.

Wayne Puny was so happy he
took the wheel off a cart and rolled it
triumphantly across the pitch. (Which
is why you often see footballers doing
cartwheels when they celebrate.)

Back in England, the celebrations commenced – but the six WAGs of Henry the 1/8th were a bit slow to join in…

"HURRY UP GIRLS, CHOP CHOP!" he shouted.

1. Catherine: too arrogant
2. Anne: bow legged
3. Jane: Need to see more?
4. Anne: Odd sleeves
5. Catherine II how 'ard?
6. Catherine III below par

And what became of Henry the 1/8th?
Well, that's another story…

DAVE WOODS
CHRIS INNS

SHORT JOHN SILVER	978 1 40831 359 6
SIR LANCE-A-LITTLE	978 1 40831 360 2
ROBIN HOODIE	978 1 40831 364 0
JUNIOR CAESAR	978 1 40831 362 6
FLORENCE NIGHTINGIRL	978 1 40831 363 3
HENRY THE 1/8TH	978 1 40831 361 9

All softbacks priced at £4.99

Orchard Books are available from all good bookshops,
or can be ordered from our website: www.orchardbooks.co.uk,
or telephone 01235 827702, or fax 01235 827703.